eISBN: 978-1-5324-1553-1
Paperback ISBN: 978-1-5324-1554-8
Hardcover ISBN: 978-1-5324-1555-5

Published in the United States by Xist Publishing
www.xistpublishing.com
PO Box 61593 Irvine, CA 92602

xist Publishing

Download a free eBook copy of this book using this QR code.

or at http://xist.pub/3c8fb

* Limited time only
Your name and a valid email address are required to download.
Must be redeemed by persons over 13

Little Hoo Goes Camping

FOR PAYAM

Brenda Ponnay

It's vacation time
for the Hoo family!

What's wrong Little Hoo?
Are you afraid to go camping?

Don't be afraid,
Little Hoo.

You are going to have so much fun!

What's wrong little Hoo?
Are the winding roads making
your tummy feel funny?

Don't worry, Little Hoo, we're almost there! Let's stop for a little bit and get some fresh air.

Are you worried
we will have no place to sleep?

Don't worry. Little Hoo,
that's why we have a tent!

What's wrong, Little Hoo?
Are you having trouble
setting up the tent?

Don't worry, Little Hoo.
Mama Hoo is an expert at setting up a tent.

What's wrong, Little Hoo?

Are you feeling hungry?

Don't worry, Little Hoo
It's time to make a fire
and roast some dinner!

Don't worry, Little Hoo.
You're going to love dessert!

Don't worry, Little Hoo.

We can wash up in this water!

What's wrong, Little Hoo?

Are you afraid of spiders hiding?

Don't worry, Little Hoo.

Spiders make a tasty snack (for owls)!

What's wrong, Little Hoo?

Are you afraid to sleep in the dark?

Don't worry, Little Hoo.
That's why we have flashlights.

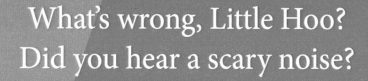

What's wrong, Little Hoo?
Did you hear a scary noise?

shuffle skuff, shuffl skuff, shuffle

What's wrong, Little Hoo?
Did you hear another scary noise?

hoooooowwwwww ooooooooooow

yip! yip! yip!

hoooooooowwwwwl!

Don't worry, Little Hoo.
It's just some neighbors celebrating!

Don't worry, Little Hoo.
We packed your favorites!

What's wrong, Little Hoo?
You aren't ready to go home?

Don't worry, Little Hoo.

We can come back again next year!